What Reggie Did On the Weekend 2

Unfair!

Lee. M. Winter

Copyright © 2016 Lee. M. Winter

All rights reserved.

ISBN-13: 978-1534606289

ISBN-10: 1534606289

CONTENTS

I Had Nothing to Do

On the weekend I did nothing. Seriously, I sat on a chair and stared at the wall. Well, that's not entirely true. After I did nothing all weekend, I wrote a song about how I did nothing all weekend.

It goes to the tune of "*The Wheels on the Bus*"

On the weekend I had nothing to do,
nothing to do, nothing to do,
On the weekend I did nothing but a
poo, all weekend long.

I stared at the wall and picked my
nose, picked my nose, picked my nose.
I stared at the wall and picked my
nose, all weekend long. (Actually, I
only did that for about five minutes).

A fly on the wall stared at me, stared
at me, stared at me,
A fly on the wall stared at me, and
watched me pick my nose.

I wondered if flies can pick their own
noses, pick their own noses, pick their
own noses,

I wondered if flies can pick their own noses, do flies even have noses?

I thought really hard about Googling 'flies', Googling 'flies', Googling 'flies', I thought really hard about Googling 'flies', and seeing if they have noses.

But Lon came along and squashed the fly, squashed the fly, squashed the fly,
Lon came along and squashed the fly, there were fly guts everywhere. (Not really everywhere, just in a smallish, banana-shaped smear).

Ma told Lon to "Clean that off, clean that off, clean that off,"
Ma told Lon to "Clean that off, and get Reggie off that chair!"

This should have been a picture of me picking my nose, but since I don't really have a nose just go ahead and use your imagination.

Running Away

On the weekend I ran away from home.

Okay, I *tried* to run away from home.

Now that I think about it, I was on my skateboard so perhaps I should say I rode away from home.

Can you run away from home without actually running? What if you pack your bags and walk away really fast? Would that still count as running away? What about hopping?

Sorry, back to the story.

It all started when I asked Ma if I could stay up late to watch a movie on TV and she said no.

I said that wasn't fair because my brothers, Ron, Con, Lon, Don, and Jon were all allowed to stay up late.

She said I was younger than them and needed more sleep.

I said I did not.

She said I did.

I said, what if I have a nap tomorrow?

She said no.

I pointed out that tomorrow was Sunday and I could sleep in.

She said no.

I said that if she let me stay up late just this once, then I'd never, ever, ever, ever, ever, ever, ever ask again.

She said no.

I stamped my foot.

She said no.

I yelled.

She said no.

I cried.

She said no.

I lay on the floor and screamed.

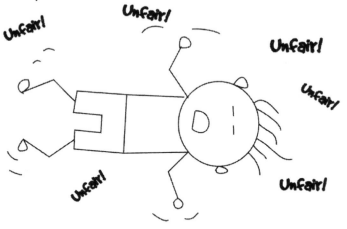

She said no.

I got up from the floor and said that if she didn't let me stay up late, I'd run away.

She said "Don't forget your jacket."

I said I really meant it.

She said "See you when you get back."

I said I wasn't coming back.

She said, "Then this is goodbye."

I stomped to my room and began stuffing clothes into my backpack. I called out "I'm packing a bag!"

She called back, "Okay!"

She was bluffing. I knew she'd never let me walk out of the house with my bag.

She watched me walk out of the house with my bag.

"Goodbye," I said, before closing the door.

"Reggie, wait!"

I knew it! I knew she wouldn't let me go. I turned to look at her.

"You forgot this," she said, holding out my jacket.

I took the jacket, walked out the door and let it bang behind me.

I stood on the front porch. I didn't really, truly want to run away. It was cold on the porch and where would I sleep? Still, it was too late to turn around now.

I put my backpack on my back, grabbed my skateboard and walked down the path and through the gate.

I glanced at the house. Ma was watching me through a window. She waved. I rode away without waving back.

At the end of the street I stopped. Now what? What do runaways do when they get to the end of the street? Suddenly, the world seemed very big and I felt very small.

Cars roared past. A bus splashed water from a puddle all over my shoes. A scary bird looked at me.

I turned and rode my skateboard back to the house as fast as I could. I walked in, went to my room and began unpacking.

Ma came in. She said, "I thought you were running away."

I said, "I can't."

She said, "Why not?"

I said, "Because I'm not allowed to cross the street by myself. But just you wait. As soon as I'm old enough to cross the street, I'm out of here. I'm totally running away and I'm going to find a family that lets me stay up late. I do NOT need more sleep than Ron, Con, Lon, Don, and Jon!"

As soon as Ma left I lay down on my bed and had a nap.

Almost running away is exhausting.

Hot Ear

On the weekend, I had a bad case of hot-ear.

For no reason whatsoever, my left ear heated up and turned bright red. This happens to me sometimes but this weekend was the worst ever.

I was like Rudolph the Red-Nosed Reindeer except I was Reggie, the red-eared boy.

We tried to cool it down but nothing worked. Ma fanned it, Dad blew on it and I rubbed it with ice but it stayed red and hot.

It glowed so red that Dad used me as a flashlight when he took out the rubbish.

Ma used me as a lamp while she read a book.

Con came in from outside and warmed his hands over it.

Lon toasted marshmallows.

There was a knock at the door and a team of government officials swarmed in. They said my ear was so red and hot that it could be seen from space. They had satellite pictures to prove it. My ear was contributing to global warming, they said. I wasn't sure what that meant but they said it was bad.

A helicopter landed in the front yard. The government officials said they were taking me to some very important people who would work out what to do about my ear.

Dad and I flew in the helicopter to New York City. In New York City we were put into a very long, very fancy car called a lima-bean. We drove in the very fancy lima-bean car to the United Nations where all the bosses of the world live.

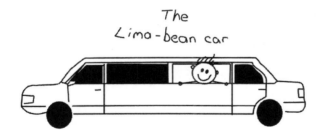

The
Lima-bean car

The bosses of the world looked at my ear and some scientists did some special tests on it, like to see just how hot it was and stuff like that.

The scientists and bosses of the world were all very happy. They said that the heat coming from my ear was enough to keep everyone in the world warm. Nobody would need to use fossil fuels anymore. I wasn't sure what that meant but they said it was good. I was going to save the planet.

Dad and I were taken to a very fancy hotel while the scientists and bosses of the world worked out how to use my ear to heat the world.

Then a bad thing happened. My ear cooled down. It stopped being red. It stopped being hot.

The scientists and bosses of the world didn't want my ear anymore.

They made us take the bus home.

Ma's Birthday Cake

On the weekend it was Ma's birthday. She went out to get her hair done so I decided to surprise her by making a birthday cake.

I searched online for 'cakes' and found a recipe. So far so good.

Even though I thought it was a little strange, I added the can of tuna and the chilli pepper to the bowl, just as the recipe said. Ma likes unusual food so I knew she'd *love* this.

Jon came into the kitchen and told me I was a dork because the recipe was for *fish* cakes, not a 'cake', cake.

This was a helpful tip.

I thanked Jon and looked for another recipe. I found one for cheesecake. It looked good. I knew Ma would love it.

The recipe said to use 'creamed cheese' but I couldn't find any in the fridge. Luckily, I did find an old bit of hard cheese right up the back that I think had been forgotten about. It had green spots on it which was perfect because green is Ma's favorite color.

Even better, 'green cheese' rhymes with 'creamed cheese' so, you know, close enough.

I threw the green cheese into the bowl with the fish and chilli. (Ma hates waste, so I knew she'd be proud of me for not wasting the fish and chilli).

I stirred it all up.

Next, Con came into the kitchen and said that all cakes need flower and eggs.

backyard and sat it in the sun for three hours hoping this would help.

What do you think happened next?
   a. We ate the cake at Ma's birthday dinner. Everyone loved it and asked for seconds.
   b. We ate the cake at Ma's birthday dinner. Everyone got sick and had to be rushed to hospital, or...
   c. Ma thought the cake was too good to eat so she entered it in a cake competition and it won first place.

Well, the answer would have been 'a' except that next door's goat came through the fence, ate the cake, got sick and had to be rushed to hospital.

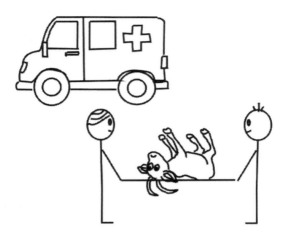

Having My Toenails Cut

On the weekend I had to go through one of the worst, most terrible, terrifying ordeals it's possible to go through. That's right –
I HAD TO HAVE MY TOENAILS CUT!!!

I *hate* having my toenails cut. In fact, I don't just hate it. I *loathe* it. I *detest* it. I *despise* it. I (*insert your own bad word here*) it!

Just the thought of Ma coming at my delicate, pink little piggy-wiggies with those tiny, shiny, pointy, razor-sharp scissors makes me break into a cold sweat.

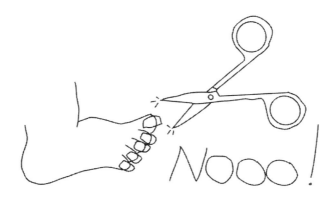

I'd probably be okay about it if I was allowed to do the cutting myself, but the problem is that Ma doesn't trust me with scissors. (I'm not sure why not. I think the curtains look better with holes.)

I'd managed to avoid it for weeks, but finally my toenails were so long they reached right down over the ends of my toes and touched the floor.

They made a funny tippity-tap noise as I walked across the kitchen tiles.

Tippity-tap, tippity-tap.
"What's that noise?" asked Ma.

I thought fast. "Er...rain on a tin roof?"

"We don't have a tin roof," said Ma. "Reggie, show me your toenails."

NOOOOOOOO!! I screamed, silently inside my head.

Ma looked at my toenails and said, "When you've finished your chores today, I'm cutting those toenails."

"*NOOOOOOO!!*" I screamed, loudly outside my head.

I tried to breathe slowly. I could get out of this. All I had to do was come up with enough chores so that by the time I was done Ma would have forgotten all about my toenails.

I cleaned my room, including in the wardrobe and under the bed.

I sorted and folded all of my socks and undies.

I sorted and folded all of Con's socks and undies.

I ran away from Con when he chased me for touching his socks and undies.

I sat down and made "WANTED" posters for all of my missing socks (I'd noticed that I was missing *a lot*. Where do they go?? I mean, you start with a red pair, a white pair, a blue pair, and a stripy pair, and end up with one red sock, one white sock, one blue sock, one stripy sock, and a weird brown sock that you've never seen before. It's maddening!)

I walked around the house looking for good places to put up my WANTED posters.

Ma said, "Reggie, are you done yet?"

"No, not yet," I said as I sticky-taped a poster to the wall over the washing machine (best to start where they were last seen).

With all of my WANTED posters up, I scratched my head and desperately tried to think of more chores to do.

I flossed my teeth.
I flossed the dog's teeth.
I cleaned my belly button.
I cleaned the dog's belly button. (At least, I hope it was his belly button. Do dogs have belly buttons?)

I sorted all my Lego into neat piles according to size and shape.

I sorted all the fruit and vegetables in the crisper according to size and shape.

I headed out back to sort all the leaves in the garden by size and shape.

"That's enough sorting, Reggie. It's nail cutting time!" called Ma.

I pretended not to hear and walked faster, but she grabbed me at the kitchen door, forced me to the ground and sat on me.

"It doesn't have to be like this, Reggie," she said, waving the tiny, shiny, pointy, razor-sharp scissors around with one hand while the other one had hold of my right ankle.

"Yes, it does!" I said.

"What are you afraid of, Reggie?" she asked, scissors ready for snipping.

"Oh, nothing much," I said, "Just that you might *CUT OFF A TOE!*"

She told me not to be ridiculous. She said that the chance of her cutting off a toe was really quite slim.

Slim? SLIM?

"SO YOU'RE ADMITTING THERE'S A *SLIM* CHANCE I COULD LOSE A TOE HERE?"

I clenched my eyes tight shut and braced for it.

Snip, snip, snip, snip, snip, snip, snip, snip, snip, snip!

"There, all done," said Ma, climbing off me.

Still lying on the floor, I was about to stand up and count my toes when something caught my eye. From down here I could see underneath the fridge. There was something blue under there.

Wait! *Was that one of my missing socks!*

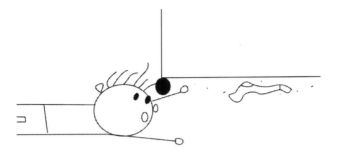

The Big Sock Hunt

On the weekend I went sock hunting.

I spent all week planning it. I'd seen my missing blue sock under the fridge *last* weekend.

I tried to grab it at the time but I couldn't get my hand into the narrow space. I ran and got the broom hoping I could push the sock out with the broom handle.

But when I came back with the broom,

the sock was gone!

That meant only one thing. The sock had made a run for it. It *knew* I was coming and it had gotten out of there fast. And what's worse, I'm pretty sure it wasn't alone. I'm pretty sure I saw something red and possibly something stripy. The socks had teamed up to form a gang.

Who knew that socks could be so cunning!

After planning all week, I was ready. I pulled on my old khaki shorts and a matching t-shirt (because that's what hunters wear) and I searched through the garage and found Lon's old fishing net.

I was now officially *The Sock Hunter.* I started saying "crikey" a lot.

I started with the fridge. Down on my hands and knees I peered underneath. As I suspected, the socks hadn't returned.

There was nothing under the fridge but a couple of fluffy dust bunnies. They looked at me. I asked them if they'd seen the socks.

"They went that way," said one of the dust bunnies, pointing out the kitchen door.

I went through the kitchen door and into the family room. I looked around and thought, now where would I hide if I were a sock? A *sneaky* sock.

On my hands and knees again I looked under all of the furniture. I found a missing Lego guy, half a chocolate chip cookie, a used tissue, and an old pair of underpants I hadn't seen for months.

"You looking for the socks?" asked the underpants.

"How did you know?" I said.

"I saw the posters."

Great! My WANTED posters were working.

The underpants told me to try the study.

I tiptoed into the study. No sense in warning them I was coming.

All was quiet. Ma's computer sat on her desk. All her paperwork was neat and tidy. The filing cabinet stood at attention.

I tried to look tough and waved the net about. "Listen up socks! I know you're in here. The jig's up. Come out now with your...er...hands up!"

Nothing.

Maybe they weren't in here after all. I was about to leave when suddenly I smelt something. *Sniff, sniff.*

Yes! My own stinky sock smell! I'd know it anywhere! It comes from own stinky feet after all. But this stink wasn't coming from my feet. It was coming from behind the filing cabinet.

Sniffing hard, I sneaked around the left side of the cabinet.

"Gotchya!" I yelled, in time to see the stripy sock disappear around the right side of the cabinet.

I ran to cut it off but wasn't fast enough. I came out from behind the cabinet to see the entire sock gang hopping straight out the door.

"Wait! Come back!" I called, "We can talk about this!"

The stripy sock gave an evil laugh, and called back, "Never! We're free, we're free! You won't catch us!"

I scooped them all up with the fishing net.

"Darn it," said the stripy sock. I asked if that was a sock joke (*Darn* it – get it?) but the sock didn't get it.

"What did you have to go and do that for?" said Stripy, who appeared to be the leader.

"Well, because you're *my* socks," I said. "You've each left an identical sock behind in my socks and undies drawer, but I can't wear socks that don't match."

"Why not?" asked Stripy.

"Well, because...because...hmmm." I couldn't think of a good answer.

"Because I just can't. Why are *you* all running away?"

Stripy sighed. "You don't know what it's like to be a sock. Either shoved in a dark drawer or stretched over a foot and stuffed into a shoe! You can't see anything from inside a shoe."

I said, "But you do get to hang on the line sometimes."

"Yes," agreed Stripy, "and the view is great from up there but we want to see more of the world. Right, boys?" The other socks all nodded.

"But what about your partners?" I said, "The other socks left in the drawer?"

Stripy shrugged. "They were too scared to come with us. Don't want to leave the drawer unless it's on a foot."

Hmmm. I thought hard about what to do. I felt sorry for the socks, I really did. I know *I* wouldn't like to be stuffed in a shoe all day, but what could I do?

Then I came up with a great idea. I asked the socks, "What if I wear sandals more often? Then, you'll be able to see everything."

The socks took a moment to discuss this amongst themselves. Finally, Stripy looked up. "It's a deal!" he said.

The socks all went back to the drawer, happy.

See what happens when you compromise? Everyone wins.

Unfair!

On the weekend I was beaten up by my brothers for wearing socks with sandals.

Helping Old People

On the weekend Ma asked me why I was wearing odd socks. I told her not to worry about that right now. What I needed right now was advice.

I belong to Little Rangers. Little Rangers is kind of like Scouts.

You meet with other kids once a week, in a hall, and learn stuff and do stuff and sometimes you go on camps where you learn and do more stuff.

Sometimes when you do stuff they give you badges.

I was trying to earn my 'Community Service' badge. To earn my badge I had to do something good in the community, but I didn't know what I could do.

Ma suggested I help old Mrs Carter, next door. "There she is, about to cross the road," said Ma, peering out the window. "Go and help her cross the road, Reggie."

Too easy.

I ran outside and pulled Mrs Carter across the road. I say 'pulled' because her legs didn't seem to work very well (maybe that's why she uses a cane). She was very heavy and I had to pull hard to get her across.

When we got to the other side she hit me over the head with her cane.

She said she hadn't wanted to cross the road. She'd been waiting for a bus.

While she was hitting me, the bus drove past.

Now she'd missed the bus.

I asked her if she wanted help getting back across the road but she said she would hit me again if I didn't go away immediately.

I went back home and told Ma what had happened. She said I should try again, this time with our other neighbour, old Mr Bennet.

Mr Bennet answered my knock at the door and invited me in. He seemed very pleased when I offered to help him with whatever he needed doing.

He told me he had to go and put his teeth in (sometimes old people keep their teeth in a glass) but in the meantime could I please go and ride on the goat?

Huh? *Ride on the goat?*

This wasn't what I'd expected but I thought, well, if that's what he wants, then sure, why not? (You remember the goat, right? The one that came through the fence and ate Ma's cake and the potato baby?)

I went out the back and climbed on the goat and did my best to ride it.

The goat didn't like it very much and kept trying to throw me off, but I held onto its horns and somehow stayed on. I rode it around the yard.

The goat started to make loud goat noises.

Mr Bennet came running outside and shouted at me to get off the goat. He was angry. So was the goat.

Get off the goat!

It turned out that Mr Bennet can't talk very well without his teeth in. I thought he'd said:

'go and ride on the goat' when what he'd really said was 'go and widen the moat'.

I double checked that his teeth were definitely in because 'widen the moat' sounded even weirder than 'ride on the goat'.

But Mr Bennet said he absolutely wanted his moat widened, handed me a shovel and stomped inside.

I looked around. Mr Bennet didn't *have* a moat. A moat is like a river of water around a castle. At least, I think it is. There was no river of water in sight.

I started to think that maybe Mr Bennet was a bit confused. I left the shovel with the goat and went home. I'm pretty sure the goat was happy to see me go.

Ma said I should try one last time and suggested I go and see Mrs Forrest three doors down.

I knocked very loudly on Mrs Forrest's door because she is a little deaf.

"Do you need any help?" I asked when she came to the door.

"Felt? No, I don't need any felt,' she said, looking puzzled. "Why would I need felt?"

"Not *felt, HELP,*" I said, loudly.

"Oh, help. Why do you need help?" She looked around as though there might be a fire nearby.

I tried again. "No," I said, "*I* don't need any help. I'm here to help *you*."

"Oh, then why didn't you say so?" She invited me in.

She told me she'd been in the middle of rearranging the books on her bookshelf. She'd taken them all down and was now putting them back up.

I said, "Can I help with that?"

"Cat? No, I don't have a cat," she said.

I said, " *That*, not *cat*."

"The cat's not fat? What are you talking about? I told you I don't have a cat, fat or thin. In fact, I'm allergic to cats. There'd better not be a cat in here." Mrs Forrest started hunting around for the cat that didn't exist.

When she couldn't find the cat, she said it would be very nice if I would please weed her vegetable garden.

At last, something I could help with.

I went outside to the vegetable garden and started pulling up the weeds. Some of them had long, orange roots that looked a lot like carrots.

Mrs Forrest came out and yelled at me to stop pulling out her carrots.

I tried to put the carrots back in the garden but before I could, Mr Bennet's goat turned up and ate them all.

Mr Bennet followed the goat in and yelled at me because I hadn't widened his moat like he'd asked AND I'd left the gate open and the goat had escaped.

I went home feeling unhappy. I wasn't going to get my Community Service badge.

Or so I thought.

Later that day, Mrs Carter, Mr Bennet, and Mrs Forrest all came over to our house. They told Ma that they were happy to say I'd helped them, if I promised to never, ever try and help them again. They said that would be the best service I could ever give to the community.

Ruining Stella's Party

On the weekend I ruined Stella's birthday party.

I didn't mean to but sometimes things just happen. Like...

My wobbly tooth fell out and my gum bled all over the presents.

Holding onto my tooth, I helped myself to a glass of fruit punch. While I was getting the punch I dropped my tooth and couldn't find it anywhere.

I thought someone might have stolen my tooth, you know, to cash in with the tooth fairy.

To find out, I made Stella and the guests stand against a wall while I searched their pockets.

And in their ears.

And up their noses.

I didn't find the tooth.

We played pin the tail on the donkey and I accidently pinned the tail to Stella's grandmother. The grandmother screamed and so did Stella.

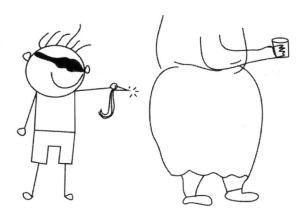

(This one happens to me a lot. Although it's not always a Grandmother. I've pinned tails on Aunts, an Uncle, a dog, a parrot and once, a goldfish. Warning – if you blindfold me, give me a sharp pin and ask me to stick it somewhere, you've only got yourself to blame when it all goes horribly wrong.)

Stella got a glass of fruit punch and started screaming again – my tooth was bobbing around in her punch alongside the cherries and pineapple chunks.

When she took a breath between screams I asked her if I could please have my tooth back.

She threw it at me. Luckily it missed.

Unluckily, it landed in the mouth of her yawning grandmother who swallowed it.

Thankfully, there was nothing left to do but sing "Happy Birthday" and eat the cake.

I accidently farted and blew out the candles.

No one wanted any cake. Except me. I ate a huge piece.

As Stella's Dad pulled me outside by my arm, I tried to give my address to her grandma so she'd know where to send the tooth-fairy money, but I'm not sure she heard me.

She'd better not think she's keeping the money.

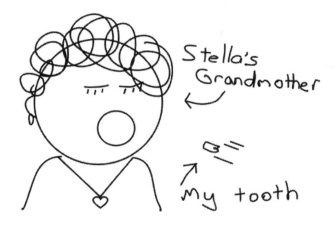

Stella's
Grandmother
←

← My tooth

The Unflushable

On the weekend I did an unflushable,
It simply would not go down,
No matter how much I pushed the
button,
It just swirled round and round.

With no other choice I called out for
Ma,
"Ma, you have to come and see!"
She said, "What have you done now,
Reggie?"

I said, "Well, I'm in the bathroom and
it starts with P!"

"Oh no, is it another unflushable?"
"Yep, you'd better come and look."
Ma stared into the bowl,
Her head just shook and shook.

We took turns to flush it
I counted every try,
We got to ninety-seven,
Before it finally said goodbye!

If I Had a Time Machine

On the weekend I thought about how great it would be to have a time machine so I could travel back in time and do a few things differently. This is what I would do:

- I would *not* shave off all of the cat's hair because she looked hot.

- I would *not* try to stick the hair back on with superglue because she looked cold.

- I would *not* announce that I don't want to kiss Great Aunt Gertie when she arrives because her beard is prickly and she smells funny when she has in fact already arrived and is standing behind me.

- I would *not* eat my glue stick in class just because Mitchell Moore ate his and said it was tasty.

- I probably *would* still eat Con's Easter eggs that he hid at the back of the wardrobe and thought I didn't know about, but I *would* run faster when he found out.

- I would *not* make myself vomit just to see if I could.

- I would *not* hold my breath until my face was the same shade of purple as the curtains just to see if I could.

- I would *not* feed the gold fish chocolate milk.

- I *would* believe Ma when she told me that boys can't fly even when they are wearing superman suits.

- I would *not* believe Lon, Ron, Don, Jon, and Con when they told me that was usually true, however *my* superman suit had been dusted with special magic flying powder given to them by a wizard who said it only works if you jump from the very top of the tree.

Ha ha!.

Getting Out of the Spelling Test

On the weekend I was very worried about the spelling test coming up on Monday.

I knew I should have learnt the words on my list but, well, I meant to sit down and learn them, I really, truly did, but I was busy with...you know...stuff. And then it was, like, too late to learn them.

Well, okay, it probably wasn't too late but by then I was panicked and stressed and in no fit state to learn anything.

So...I came up with a clever plan to get out of sitting the test.

To get out of sitting the test I would have to not be at school, unless I could get Ma to write a note to say I was allergic to spelling and could I please be excused from the test.

Even I didn't really think that Ma would go for that, so I went to plan B.

I would have to make Ma believe I was sick. Too sick to go to school.

First of all, sick people feel hot.

To make myself hot I put on my thermal underwear, two pairs of pants, thick socks, my ski jacket, and a scarf and sat in my room until I felt sweat trickle down my back.

I stripped off the extra clothes and while I was still hot, quickly ate some cold, cooked, limp, slimy cabbage I'd taken earlier from the fridge. I just made it into the kitchen in time to puke up the cabbage (along with the chocolate milkshake and hot dog I'd had for lunch) all over the floor.

It was great!

Ma stepped over the puke pile and felt my forehead.

"Reggie, you're burning up. Get into bed.

Great! She was buying it. Ma really thought I was sick.

I got into bed.

She came in and took my temperature. She said I had a fever. Things were going well.

I said, "So, I'll have to miss school tomorrow, right?"

Ma said, "Maybe not."

MAYBE NOT?

"But I'm sick! I've got a *TEMPERATURE*!"

Ma said, "Stay in bed. I'll check your temperature later and then again in the morning. If it goes back to normal then off to school you go."

Oh no. This meant I had to keep myself hot. As soon as Ma left the room I put back on the two pairs of pants, thick socks, my ski jacket, and scarf and climbed back under the blankets.

I was hot.

Still, I wasn't sure if I would be hot enough so I sneaked into the bathroom and filled a hot-water bottle with hot water and took it back to bed with me.

I snuggled down under the blankets and cuddled the hot-water bottle.

I was hot.

Very hot.

I wondered how long it would be before Ma came to check my temperature.

The sweat didn't trickle down my back, it ran like a river. The sweat river rolled down my back, between my butt cheeks, down each leg and into my socks.

Sweat puddle

Half an hour passed. Then an hour. Still Ma didn't return. I lost track of time. My clothes were soaked with sweat, the blankets were soaked with sweat, and my bedroom was filling up with sweat. I kind of fell asleep and dreamed I was being washed away in a river. A HOT, sweaty river.

Things got so bad that I started to feel sick for real. And slightly weird in the head. I couldn't remember my name or why I was so hot. *WHY WAS I SO HOT? Why was I floating away on a river?*

After that, everything is fuzzy. I kind of remember Ma coming in, pulling the blankets and clothes off me and putting me in a cool bath.

I think a doctor came and looked at me because I heard someone tell Ma I was DEHYDRATED and needed to go to hospital. I'm not sure what 'dehydrated' means but I went to hospital and spent the night there.

The next morning they said I was all better but should stay home from school that day.

YAY! I'd done it! I was so clever: My plan had worked and I wouldn't have to sit the spelling test!

I'm so clever,
I'm the best,
I'm smarter than all the rest!

That afternoon, my friend Jimmy stopped by to find out why I hadn't been at school. He said it had been Bring-Your-Skateboard-And-Have-Free-Ice-cream-Day and I'd missed it.

The spelling test was tomorrow.
Sad face.

Driving Ma Mad

On the weekend it was raining so I had to stay inside with Ma. I drove her mad.

I don't mean angry-mad, I mean crazy-mad.

By the time I'd finished with her she was completely and totally barking mad. I heard actual barks as she ran away down the road. Unless that was the dog across the street that barks whenever anyone runs by, especially mad mothers. Hard to say.

It was the questions that drove her mad. I spent the first four hours, thirty-seven minutes and twenty-three seconds of the morning asking questions.

Ma, when is Aunt Josie coming to stay?

Next Thursday.

Why isn't she coming on Wednesday?

Because she works on Wednesday.

Where does she work?

In an office.

What's an office?

A place where people work at desks with computers.

Do you need a desk to have a computer?

No.

Where would you put your computer if you didn't have a desk?

I guess you'd have to hold it.

Wouldn't that get heavy? What if you dropped it on your toe?

Then you would have a sore toe.

Would it break your toe?

It might.

Then shouldn't the office boss make sure everyone has a desk?

They probably do.

But you said you didn't need to have a desk.

I was wrong. You need a desk.

So everyone has one?

Reggie, please stop asking questions!

Why? What's wrong with questions?

Nothing, but you ask too many.

How many should I ask?

No more than three.

Is that the law?

It should be.

Well, do you mean three a day, or three a minute, or three for my whole life?

I can live with three per day.

That's not many, is it?

No.

Can I ask *you* three questions and *Dad* another three questions or is it three questions all up?

Three each.

What about at school? How many questions can I ask there?

REGGIE!! STOP! YOU'RE DRIVING ME MAD!!

Sorry, Ma. I love you.

I love you, too, Reggie.

Ma?

Yes, Reggie?

When you drive someone mad you don't actually do any driving, do you? I mean, you don't put them in a car and drive them anywhere. It's an odd saying, don't you think, Ma? Why do we say 'driving someone mad', Ma?

Ma?

Ma, come back! It's raining outside; don't you think you should take an umbrella? MA! UMBRELLA IS A WEIRD WORD, ISN'T IT, MA? WHY DO WE CALL THEM UMBRELLAS, MA? MA, ARE YOU BARKING OR IS THAT THE DOG ACROSS THE STREET?

Driving Dad Mad

On the weekend I drove Dad mad. I
don't mean angry-mad, I mean crazy-
mad. Only he didn't bark like a dog.
When Dad goes crazy-mad he grinds
his teeth together and a small muscle
on the side of his head moves in and
out.

I started working on him at lunch time
and finished him off in the afternoon.

It started when he said:

Reggie, come and eat your lunch. I've made you a chicken sandwich.

Thanks, Dad, but I can't eat chicken sandwiches.

What? Why not? You love chicken sandwiches.

No, I used to love chicken sandwiches. I don't anymore.

Reggie, you've insisted on having a chicken sandwich for lunch every day for the past two months.

What's your point?

If you loved chicken sandwiches yesterday, why can't you eat one today?

Because at the moment I'm only eating yellow food.

Yellow food?

That's right.

What, like bananas?

Yes, like bananas. Do we have any bananas?

No.

Pineapple?

No.

Cheese?

No.

Well, can we go to the supermarket and buy some bananas, pineapple, and cheese?

No.

Have you got *anything* that's yellow?

Um...yes! Corn on the cob! You can have corn on the cob with butter on top, and butter's yellow so that's perfect!

Sorry, Dad can't do it.

Why not?

I don't like corn on the cob. And anyway, corn on the cob is a vegetable and vegetables aren't included in the yellow thing. When it comes to vegetables I'm only eating blue ones right now.

REGGIE! JUST EAT THE CHICKEN SANDWICH!!

After we'd been to the supermarket and I'd eaten my lunch of bananas, pineapple and cheese, I went with Dad to run an errand in the next town. We drove there in Dad's car.

Are we there yet?

No.

Are we there yet?

No.

Are we there yet?

No.

The drive to the town took thirty minutes. I asked 'are we there yet' 462 times.

This was a personal best. My previous PB was 431 and I was really proud of myself for beating it. Dad says I should always try my best at everything I do.

Finally, we got there.

Dad?

Yes, Reggie?

I need to go to the bathroom.

Why didn't you go before we left?

I didn't need to go then.

(Sigh). Okay, there's a bathroom here. Come on.

Dad, it's smelly in here.

Just hurry up and go.

I can't go if it's smelly.

Yes, you can, just hold your nose.

Dad?

Yes, Reggie?

Can you please hold my nose for me?

What? Why?

Because I have to do a number two.

So?

Well, I won't be able to wipe properly if I have to hold my nose at the same time.

Grrrr...Okay, just hurry up.

Dad?

Yes, Reggie?

Can you please hold my shoes and socks?

What? Why?

Because when I do number twos I have to take off my shoes and socks and –

Why on earth do you have to take off your shoes and socks?

I just do. It's complicated.

Okay, Reggie, I'm holding your nose and I'm holding your shoes and socks. Can you please hurry up?

Dad?

Yes, Reggie?

I don't need to go anymore, it's gone away. Dad? *Dad, come back! You've got my shoes and socks!!*

Yo-Mama

On the weekend I thought about how cool it would be if I changed my name to "Yo-Mama".

I made a list of all the different ways it would sound awesome.

When Ma calls the dentist:

"Hello? Yes, this is Mrs McDonald. I'd like to make an appointment for *Yo-Mama.*"

Being called for our turn at the Doctor:
"*Yo-Mama?*"

Then not answering so they have to call again. "*Yo-Mama? Is Yo-Mama* here?

At the park:
"*Yo-Mama!* Come down from the climbing frame, it's time to eat your snacks."

At home:
"Who ate all the chocolate chip cookies?"

"*Yo-Mama!*"

Or

"Hurry up in the bathroom! *Yo-Mama* needs to pee!"

The Snotty Kid and the Big Dog Poo

On the weekend I wrote some more poems.

There's this kid in my class,
Whose nose drips snot,
I mean, like, *always*,
I'm talking a *lot*.

It grosses me out,

I'm not being mean,

It wouldn't be so bad,

If it wasn't bright green. (Which Ma says may indicate an infection – he should see a doctor.)

It runs down his face,

Heading due South,

I try not to puke,

When it goes in his mouth.

My dog did a really big poo one day,

I showed it to my friend, Sam.

It was way too big to keep to ourselves,

So we put it on Instagram! *(And then had our account banned because that really is disgusting and you shouldn't do it!)*

Hiding Cabbage

On the weekend I made a list of the best places to hide unwanted cabbage so your mother thinks you've eaten it. You're welcome. Here's the list:

If there's only a little, under your knife.

If there's a lot, under your mashed potato. If that doesn't work:

In your pockets.

In your brother's pockets.

In your shoes.

In your armpits (seriously, I had to do this once when I was barefoot and pocketless. Just make sure to keep your arms tight against your body when you leave the table.)

Feed it to the
dog/cat/goldfish/parrot—they
probably won't take it but it's worth a
shot.

In a secret cabbage-hiding compartment you've constructed and attached to the underside of the table for just this purpose. If you use this one, don't forget to empty the compartment every now and then or the rotten cabbage stink will totally give it away.

The cabbage goes in here

Last, an oldie but a goldie – sometimes it works just to spread the cabbage around the plate a bit so it looks like you've eaten at least *some*. I call this *hiding the cabbage in plain sight*.

Good luck!

Other Books by Lee. M. Winter

Angus Adams: the adventures of a
free-range kid (Book 1)

Angus Adams and the Missing Pro
Surfer
(Book 2)

Angus Adams and Scream House
(Book 3)

WWW.LEEMWINTER.COM

Made in the USA
San Bernardino, CA
02 February 2019